BERNARD'S
BATH

BERNARD'S BATH

BY JOAN ELIZABETH GOODMAN

ILLUSTRATED BY
DOMINIC CATALANO

BOYDS MILLS PRESS

For Juliet Eve, with whom I have learned
the many pleasures of bath time
— J.G.

For my mom, who made bath time,
and the rest of my childhood, a joy!
—D.C.

Published by Bell Books
Boyds Mills Press, Inc.
A Highlights Company
815 Church Street
Honesdale, Pennsylvania 18431
Printed in China

Publisher Cataloging-in-Publication Data
Goodman, Joan Elizabeth.
       Bernard's Bath / by Joan Elizabeth Goodman ; illustrated by
Dominic Catalano.
[32]p. : col. ill. ; cm.
Summary : When a little elephant refuses to take a bath, his parents must
show him how much fun bath time can be. Pastel illustrations accompany text.
ISBN 1-56397-323-5 hc / ISBN 1-56397-854-7 pbk
1. Baths—Fiction—Juvenile literature. [2. Baths—Fiction.]
I. Catalano, Dominic, ill. II. Title.
   [E]—dc20   1996   AC
Library of Congress Catalog Card Number 95-75748

First Boyds Mills Press paperback edition, 2000
Book designed by Tim Gillner and Dominic Catalano
The text of this book is set in 20-point Galliard.
The illustrations are done in pastels.

10 9 8 7 6 5 4 3 2 1

"Bernard!" called Mama. "It's time for your bath."

Bernard was nowhere in sight.

"Come out," called Papa. "Bath time is fun time."

"No bath," said Bernard from inside the linen closet.

Grandma opened the closet door.

"All little elephants love to take baths," she said.

"I don't," said Bernard.

"But of course you do," said Mama.

Papa helped Bernard out from under the towels and brought him into the bathroom.

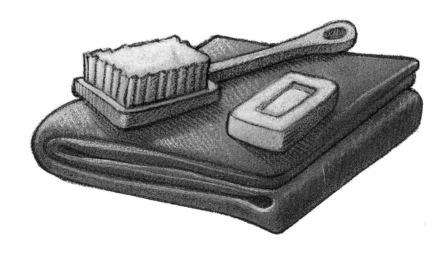

"Look, Bernard," said Papa. "Here is your nice bath. The water isn't too hot or too cold. It is just right."

"No bath," said Bernard.

"Look, Bernard," said Mama. "Bubbles for your bath." And she poured pink syrup into the tub. Soon there were mountains of bubbles.

Bernard turned away. "No bath," he said.

"Here is Duck-Duck," said Papa. "He will swim with you in your bath."

"No bath," said Bernard.

"Here is Boat to sail with you," said Grandma. "And here are cups and sponges and soap crayons."

"What a nice bath," said Mama. Mama, Papa, and Grandma looked at the bath and smiled. Bernard shut his eyes tight and frowned.

"Papa will show you," said Mama.

Papa got into the tub. He made a crown of bubbles on his head. He made big bubbly waves for Duck-Duck and Boat. Papa filled his trunk with water and sprayed himself. He lay back in the water and smiled.

"It is such a nice bath," said Mama.

"No bath," said Bernard.

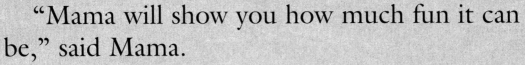

"Mama will show you how much fun it can be," said Mama.

She climbed into the tub with Papa. She soaped her trunk with pink and purple soap crayons, then dunked it underwater and trumpeted. Mama splashed Papa. Papa splashed Mama. They laughed and laughed.

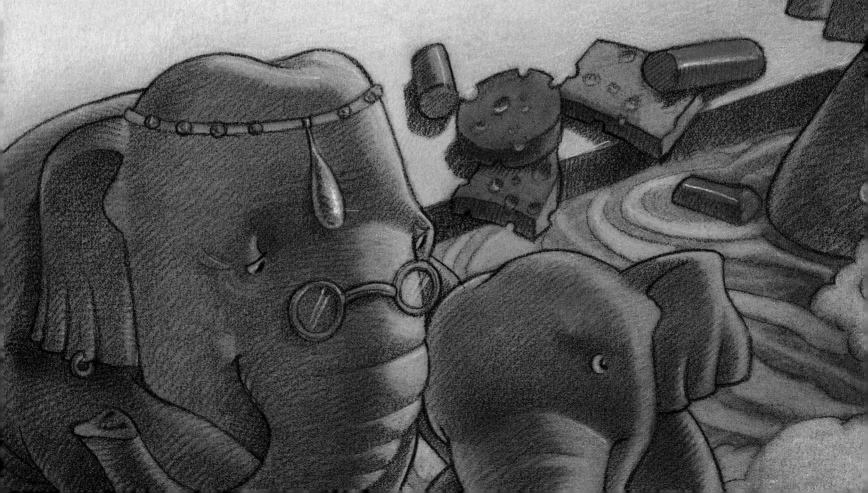

"What a fun bath," said Grandma. "I'm getting in, too."

"Wait," said Bernard.

Grandma hopped into the tub with Mama and Papa. There was a tremendous splash.

"Tidal wave!" yelled Grandma. Water sloshed all around the tub and onto the walls and floor.

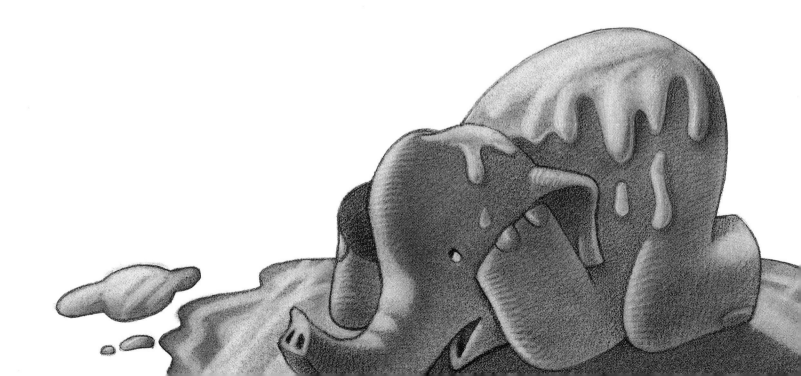

"Rub-a-dub-dub," sang Papa.

"Three trunks in a tub," sang Mama.

"And what a hubbub there was!" Grandma whooped. She raised her trunk up high and sprayed water like a fountain.

Bernard sat on the bath mat all alone.

"Maybe bath," he said.

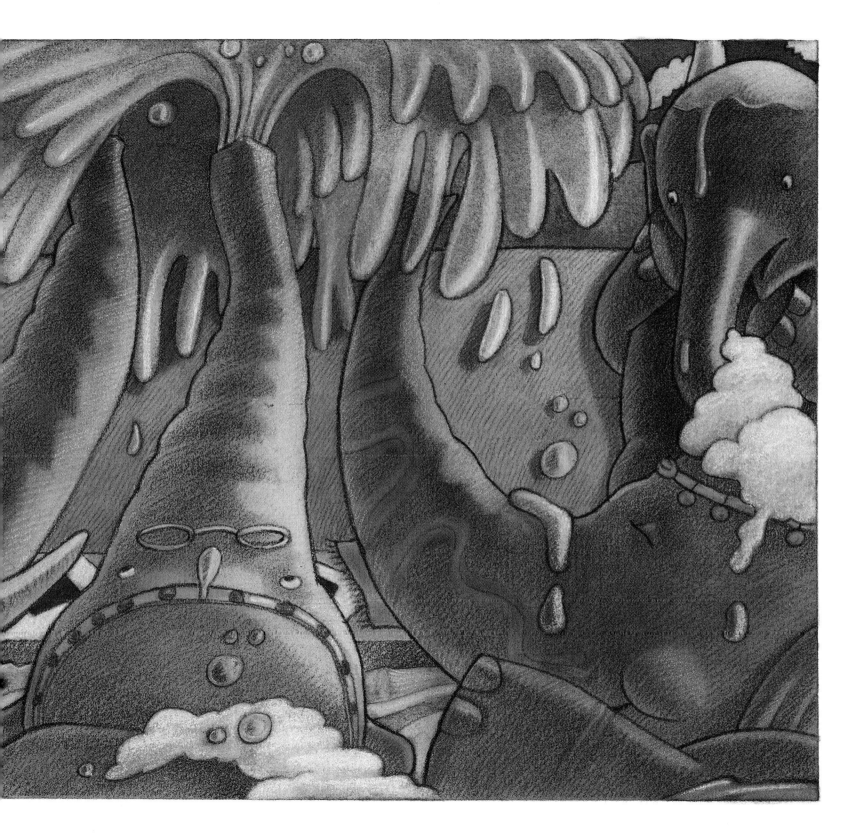

Mama, Papa, and Grandma didn't hear him. They were too busy playing divers and submarines.

"Bath," said Bernard.

Still nobody heard him.

"Splish, splash," sang Papa.

"We were taking a bath," Mama and Grandma joined in.

"BATH!" bellowed Bernard. "MY BATH!"

Papa, Mama, and Grandma stopped singing and looked at him.

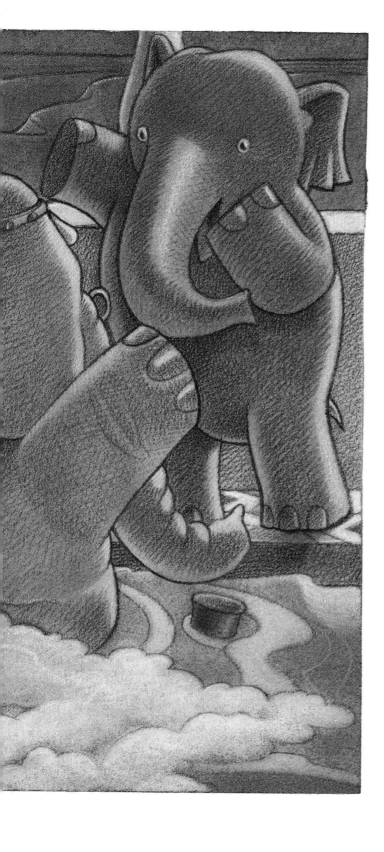

"Yes, that's right," said Mama.

"It is your bath," said Papa.

"Would you like to have your bath now?" asked Grandma.

"Yes, bath," said Bernard.

"Well, hop in," said Papa. "There is always room for one more."

And in he went. SPLASH!

"Bath!" said Bernard. "BATH!"